This book belongs to
my friend:

Saul

# A NOTE TO PARENTS

Children are first aware of the seasons in simple ways—wearing hats and mittens in winter, swimming in summer, playing in leaf piles in fall. In *Dora's Search for the Seasons*, you and your child will journey with Dora the Explorer through all the seasons.

As you read the book together, ask your child to point out visual clues to the seasons. "What season do you think it is on this page? How do you know?" Take extra time to pause on the pages that invite reader participation. For example, encourage your child to locate Swiper's hiding place in Fall Forest and find the way out of Spring Meadow before Dora does.

It is easy to continue exploring the seasons with your child. In any season, turn an everyday walk into a nature walk. Collect nature objects, such as leaves or flowers, that can be put into a seasons scrapbook. Follow animal tracks in winter, plant flowers in spring, learn to identify birds and their songs in summer, make leaf cards in fall. With a little thought, you can make every season a fun, hands-on learning adventure!

**Learning Fundamental:**  **science**

# Dora's Search for the Seasons

# ENGLISH/SPANISH GLOSSARY and PRONUNCIATION GUIDE

| English | Spanish | Pronunciation |
|---|---|---|
| Hello | Hola | OH-lah |
| It's fall | Es otoño | ES oh-TOH-nyoh |
| It's cold | Hace frío | AH-say FREE-oh |
| It's winter | Es invierno | ES een-BYEER-noh |
| It's spring | Es primavera | ES pree-mah-BEH-rah |
| It's hot. | Hace calor | AH-say cah-LOR |
| It's summer | Es verano | ES be-RAH-noh |
| Thank you | Gracias | GRAH-see-ahs |
| Good-bye | Adiós | Ah-dee-OHS |

Published by Scholastic Inc., 90 Old Sherman Turnpike, Danbury, CT 06816

SCHOLASTIC and associated logos are trademarks and/or registered trademarks of Scholastic Inc.

ISBN 0-7172-6618-4

Printed in the U.S.A.

First Scholastic Printing, September 2002

# Dora's Search for the Seasons

by
## Samantha Berger

illustrated by
## Steve Savitsky

SCHOLASTIC INC.

New York   Toronto   London   Auckland   Sydney
Mexico City   New Delhi   Hong Kong   Buenos Aires

Dora and Boots were best friends.
They shared adventures and played
together every day.

One afternoon, during a game of hide-and-seek, Dora and Boots heard someone crying. They followed the sound and found a baby flamingo.

"*Hola,* Baby Flamingo," said Dora. "Why are you so sad?"

"I flew too far from home," said Baby Flamingo. "I'm lost!"

"Where do you live?" asked Dora.

"I live with my family at Summer Lake," said Baby Flamingo, "where it's always warm and sunny."

"Don't worry," said Dora, "we'll help you get home."

But there was one problem. Dora and Boots didn't know how to get to Summer Lake. Luckily, they knew someone who could help.

"Map! Map!" Dora and Boots called. Map jumped right out of Backpack's side pocket.

"*Hola,* Map," Dora said. "We need to
get Baby Flamingo home to Summer Lake."
"No problem! I know how to get to
Summer Lake!" Map assured them.

Map continued, "First, you go through Fall Forest. Next, climb Winter Mountain. Then go across Spring Meadow. That's how you'll get to Summer Lake."

Dora and Boots repeated exactly what Map had said, "Fall Forest, Winter Mountain, Spring Meadow, Summer Lake." They were ready for their trip!

Dora, Boots, and Baby Flamingo sang as they walked along. Suddenly they came to a thick forest full of colorful trees. Leaves of red, orange, and yellow swirled all around them.

"This must be Fall Forest!" shouted Dora.
"Yes," Boots agreed, "it's fall."
Dora, Boots, and Baby Flamingo played
in the leaves—*Crunch! Crunch! Crunch!*

Dora, Boots, and Baby Flamingo picked some apples to take on their trip. They were so busy, they didn't notice Swiper the fox hiding behind a tree.

"Did you hear something?" asked Dora, looking around. Where was Swiper?

All of a sudden Swiper jumped out and tried to
swipe the apples. But Dora and Boots saw him
just in time and shouted, "Swiper, no swiping!"
Swiper stopped and snapped his fingers.
"Oh mannn!" he cried as he slunk away.
"Phew!" said Boots, "that was a close one!"

The three friends made it to the far end
of Fall Forest.

"I hope we're getting close to Summer Lake,"
said Baby Flamingo.

"Where do we go next?" asked Boots.

Dora repeated what Map had said, "Fall Forest, Winter Mountain, Spring Meadow, Summer Lake. After Fall Forest, Winter Mountain is next!"

Dora, Boots, and Baby Flamingo started climbing
Winter Mountain. It got much colder.
"*Brrrr,*" said Baby Flamingo. "This doesn't
feel like my home at Summer Lake."

Boots shivered. "What can we do to get warm?"
Dora's friend, Backpack, always had what she needed.
"Hmm," thought Dora. "What's good for staying
warm when it's cold outside?"

Dora, Boots, and Baby Flamingo each put on winter clothes. Then they continued climbing to the very top of Winter Mountain.

"¡Es invierno!"

"It's winter!"

When they reached the top, it started to snow.

"Yeah! I love winter!" Boots exclaimed.

Suddenly a snowman on top of the mountain spoke.

"If you like winter and snow, you'll love this sled!"

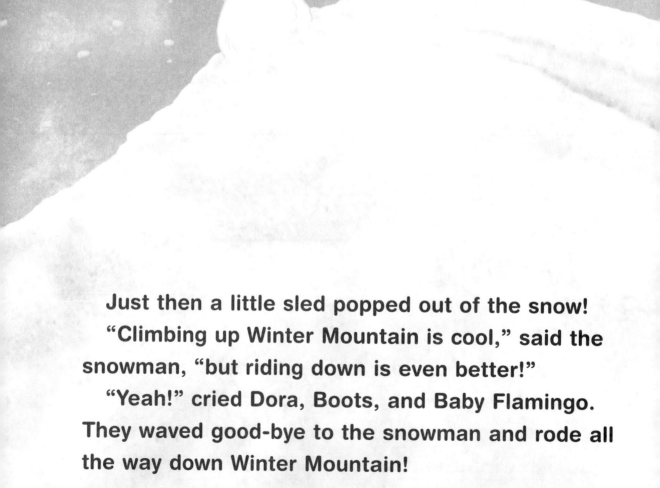

Just then a little sled popped out of the snow!
"Climbing up Winter Mountain is cool," said the
snowman, "but riding down is even better!"
"Yeah!" cried Dora, Boots, and Baby Flamingo.
They waved good-bye to the snowman and rode all
the way down Winter Mountain!

"Where do we go next?" asked Baby Flamingo when they got to the bottom.

"I know! I know!" shouted Boots. "After Winter Mountain comes Spring Meadow!"

As Dora, Boots, and Baby Flamingo walked
along towards Spring Meadow, it stopped snowing,
and the sun came out. Birds sang in their nests,
and little buds blossomed on the trees.

"¡Es primavera!"

"It's spring!"

The three friends took off their winter clothing.
"We made it to Spring Meadow," said Dora.
"But finding our way through it might be tough."

In front of them were three different paths through Spring Meadow. They wondered which one to take. One path went around a stone wall, another path went under a bridge, and another path went over a hill of flowers.

"Which path should we take?" asked Dora.
A family of frogs was crossing Spring Meadow.
"Look!" Boots shouted. "Should we follow them?"
"Yes," Baby Flamingo said happily, "there are lots
of frogs at Summer Lake!"
"Good idea," Dora said. "Which way are they going?"

The three travelers excitedly followed the frog family out of Spring Meadow. Suddenly it got much hotter. Baby Flamingo smiled and said, "We must be getting close to my home."

"Hace calor."

"It's hot."

Dora, Boots, and Baby Flamingo had hiked across Fall Forest, climbed Winter Mountain, and walked through Spring Meadow. Now, they had almost reached Summer Lake.

"It sure feels like summer here," Boots said.
"This is it! This is it!" cheered Baby Flamingo.
"This is Summer Lake."

"¡Es verano!"

"It's summer!"

There were many different animal families at
Summer Lake.

"Which one is your family?" Dora asked Baby Flamingo.

"My family looks just like me!" said Baby Flamingo.

"Hmm...," thought Dora, "which family looks just like
Baby Flamingo?"

Baby Flamingo's family came flapping and
fluttering over to Baby Flamingo. "We missed you
so much!" they all said, hugging Baby Flamingo.

"Thank you, Dora and Boots! *Gracias*," said Baby Flamingo. "I couldn't have found my way home without you."